TEENY WITCH

and
The GREAT
Halloween Ride

by LIZ MATTHEWS
illustrated by CAROLYN LOH

Troll Associates

Library of Congress Cataloging-in-Publication Data

Matthews, Liz.
    Teeny Witch and the great Halloween ride / by Liz Matthews;
illustrated by Carolyn Loh.
      p.   cm.
    Summary: Teeny Witch and her three witch aunts find an unusual way
of fulfilling witch rule 13, which states that they must ride on
Halloween night.
    ISBN 0-8167-2274-9 (lib. bdg.)   ISBN 0-8167-2275-7 (pbk.)
    [1. Halloween—Fiction. 2. Witches—Fiction. 3. Aunts—Fiction.]
I. Loh, Carolyn, ill. II. Title.
PZ7.M4337Tcr 1991
[E]—dc20   90-11207

This edition published in 2002.

"Wow!" cried Teeny Witch in surprise. "This is the biggest pumpkin I've ever seen. What a super jack-o'-lantern it will make!

Thank you, Aunts."

"Start carving it,"
urged Aunt Icky.

"Give it a scary face,"
suggested Aunt Ticky.

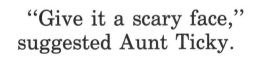

"Make it really spooky,"
said Aunt Vicky.

Carefully Teeny began to hollow out her jack-o'- lantern.
"Halloween is such a fun holiday," Teeny said.
"There are so many fun things to do."

"Halloween is special," agreed Aunt Icky.
"It's an important day for us," said Aunt Ticky.
"It's the day all the witches ride," added Aunt Vicky.

Teeny Witch stopped
working.
"Do we have to ride
tonight?" she asked.
"I don't like that part
of Halloween."

The tiny witch glanced over at her magic broom.
It really was a very nice little broom.
But she did not like flying.

"Soaring through clouds on a wobbly broom scares
me," Teeny said. "I don't like to fly."

"We don't like it either," Aunt Icky admitted.
"But we have to ride on Halloween."
Aunt Ticky nodded. "It's a rule," she said.
"That's right," agreed Aunt Vicky. "Rule 13 states witches must ride on Halloween night . . . or else."

"Or else what?" asked Teeny.

"No one knows," answered Aunt Icky.

"But you can bet it's something awful," said Aunt Ticky.

"That's why witches ride on Halloween," said Aunt Vicky. "No one wants to find out what that awful 'or else' is."

Teeny Witch sighed and carved her pumpkin's mouth into a frown.

"Oh, all right," she said. "I'll ride tonight. But I won't like it."

Aunt Ticky laughed. She went to the door. "I'm going into the garage," she said. "I have lots of work to do before tonight."

Teeny wondered what was going on. Aunt Ticky had been working in the garage for weeks. It was all very strange. But since her odd aunts always acted strange, Teeny didn't give it much thought. She just kept working on her pumpkin.

"There!" said Teeny Witch. "My jack-o'-lantern is all finished. How does it look?"

"It looks awful," said Aunt Icky. And she made a sour face.

"It's really ugly," said Aunt Vicky. "We love it!"

Teeny put her jack-o'-lantern out on the front porch. Then she went back inside to help her aunts pack treat bags. They stuffed bags with candy, cookies, taffy, gum, and other tasty things.

ding·dong·bong

When they were done, Teeny stacked the treat bags on a tray. She put the tray near the front door. The job was finished just in time.

Ding-Dong-Bong went the doorbell.

Teeny opened the door. There stood a cowboy wearing
a big hat, a pretty ballerina in a pink dress, and a
funny clown.

"Trick or treat! Stinky feet! We want something good to eat," the three trick-or-treaters shouted.

"Here are your treats," said Teeny Witch.
She gave each one a treat bag.
"Thank you," said the trick-or-treaters.

"I like your costumes," said Teeny Witch.

"Your witch costume is nice, too," said the pretty ballerina. Teeny giggled. She wasn't even wearing a costume.

"All you need is a broom to make your costume perfect," said the cowboy. "You should get one before you march in the parade tonight."

Teeny was puzzled. "What parade?" she asked.

"Don't you know about the big parade?" asked the funny clown.

Teeny shook her head.

"There is a big Halloween parade tonight," said the clown. "All the kids in town are marching in it."

The ballerina nodded. "There will be bands and floats and prizes and lots more," she said.

"The parade is a safe way for everyone to have fun on Halloween night," added the cowboy.

"I wish I could march in the parade," Teeny said.
"You can march with us," said the little clown.
"And you can trick or treat with us, too," said the
pretty ballerina.

"Hooray!" shouted Teeny.
"I'll ask my aunts if I can go."
She dashed off into the kitchen
to speak to her aunts.

"Can I go? Can I?" Teeny
asked.

Aunt Icky looked at Aunt
Vicky. Aunt Vicky looked
back at Aunt Icky.

"Well?" Teeny said.
"What is your answer?"

"Yes and no," Aunt Icky replied.

"What?" said Teeny.

"You can go trick or treating," Aunt Vicky explained. "But you can't march in the parade."

"Why not?" Teeny asked.

"Because tonight is the night witches ride," Aunt Icky reminded her.

Teeny gulped. "I forgot. I'll be back in time for our ride."

Teeny picked up her broom and joined her new friends. She told them she couldn't march in the parade with them.

"Don't be sad," said the ballerina. "Trick or treating will be lots of fun. Let's go."

Teeny Witch and her friends went from house to house. Every time a door opened they shouted, "Trick or treat!"

At a house with lots of spooky decorations they got candy bars.

At the next house, a friendly man gave them each
a shiny coin.

At another house, a nice lady gave them all packs of bubble gum.

Soon their bags were filled with all sorts of goodies.
Before long the full moon was high in the sky.
"It's almost time for the parade," said the cowboy.

"And it's time for me to go home," said Teeny.
"Good-bye, Teeny," said the ballerina.
"Good-bye and thanks," called Teeny
as she walked away.

Teeny Witch grumbled
all the way home. "I wish
there was no Rule 13," she
said. "I don't want to go for
a ride on Halloween night."

When Teeny got home she found Aunt Icky and Aunt
Vicky waiting on the porch. They had their brooms ready.

Teeny put her treat bag in the house. Then she came back out with her broom. It was then that she noticed something was missing.

"My jack-o'-lantern!" she cried. "Where is it?"

"Ask Aunt Ticky,"
said Aunt Icky.
"She's by the garage,"
said Aunt Vicky.
They both giggled as
Teeny Witch walked
toward the garage.

"Are you ready for our Halloween ride?" Aunt Ticky asked Teeny.

"Yes," said Teeny Witch with a sigh. "But where is my pumpkin?"

"We're taking it for a ride with us," laughed Aunt Ticky. And she pulled open the garage doors.

"This is what we're riding on."

Teeny Witch couldn't believe her eyes. In the garage was a Halloween float. It was scary, spooky, and wonderful. Right in the middle of the float was Teeny's giant jack-o'-lantern.

"I made it myself," said Aunt Ticky.

"That's why you couldn't march in the parade," said Aunt Icky.

"You're going to ride in the parade on this float with us," said Aunt Vicky.

"Oh boy!" shouted Teeny as they all hopped on the float. "But what about Rule 13?"

"Don't worry about that," said Aunt Icky. "The rule only says we have to ride on Halloween night."

"It doesn't say what we have to ride on," said Aunt Vicky.

"So we're all going to ride on the Halloween float,"
said Aunt Ticky. And she started the float's motor.
Zoom! Off they drove toward town.

What a great night it turned out to be!
Everyone loved the scary witch float.
Teeny even got to wave to her new friends.

It was the greatest Halloween ride of all. And the best part was . . . the witch float won first prize!

Happy Halloween!